A number of people made contributions to this book and our understanding of Peru. Our thanks go to Carlos Janela and Scott McDougall for sharing their travels and photographs. The two perspectives they offered were helpful in setting the foundation of the book.

Special thanks, however, are owed to Bron McLeod and also the Untama family, specifically Dario, Monica, and their daughter Andrea. They gave us a deeper understanding not only of Peruvian culture in general, but the many smaller cultures that it consists of. Though these are many, they all influence each other to produce an astonishingly unique nation.

As always, we wish to thank our families and friends for their support.

Amy Houston Oler

MOLLY and the Magic Suitcase

MOLLY GOES TO PERU

WRITTEN by CHRIS OLER

ILLUSTRATED by AMY HOUSTON OLER

PUBLISHED by  COLOR.
marketing & design

Hi! I'm Molly and this is my brother Michael. We find so many incredible things to explore in the world. We learn about things that are new to us, but some of them have been around a long time. Sometimes we come upon new games or dances. There is always different food and we love to find out about different languages. All sorts of things make us want to take our Magic Suitcase and explore!

"Wow! That animal is cool looking. What is it?"

"It's a llama. I raised this one and I'm showing it in the fair."

"A llama? Why is it called that?"

"I'm not sure, but they come from Peru. We raise them here now. Some even use them as guards for sheep!"

"Really? A guard llama?"

"Some llamas are very good at it."

"I want to learn more about llamas, Michael. It was so... interesting looking. It kind of looked like it was smiling."

"The girl said they're from Peru. Where should we start?"

"Let's start in the capital city again. Lima, Peru!"

"Here we go!"

"¿Cómo llegó hasta aquí?"

"I'm sorry, we don't speak much Spanish.
 I'm Molly and this is Michael."

"Hi."

"Oh, I asked how you got here. I heard a 'pop,' turned
 around, and the two of you were standing there."

"Where are we?"

"This is *El Parque del Amor.* You'd say 'Love Park,'
 and we're in Lima looking out over the Pacific Ocean."

"Molly, this reminds me a little of *Parc Güell* in Barcelona!"

"It was modeled after it. I am Cayetana."

"It's very nice to meet you. What else should
 we see in Lima?"

"I will show you around."

"This library is special. Some of the books here go back to the 1500s. There is no other place quite like this in the Americas."

"But it's not just the books, the library itself is...is...I don't know. It seems mystical, you know?"

"And like we stepped back in time, Michael."

"Hah! Yes, I'm afraid we don't appreciate it as much as we could. It is everyday stuff for us, but it is fun to hear others describe it!"

"Molly, you have *ceviche* and Michael has *flan*. Michael and I are both drinking *chicha*, a drink made from purple corn."

"What else do you like to eat, Cayetana?"

"The *ceviche* is usually very good because of how fresh the fish is here in Lima, but I really like the *lucuma*. It's not a dish, it's a fruit that kind of tastes like an orange, but less sour. It has the feel of an apple when you bite into it. It's really sweet! I could eat them all day."

"That's not what you have there, is it?"

"No, this is *olluquito*. It's sort of a small potato and it's served with meat and spices with rice."

"This is something new for Lima. There are thirteen
different fountains that make up *El Circuito Mágico del Agua*.
It means 'Magic Water Tour' and it's the largest group
of fountains in the world."

"Hah-hah! It's like a tunnel, but I'm still getting a little wet."

"Yes, Michael, this is *Fuente Túnel de las Sorpresas*,
the 'Tunnel Fountain of Surprises.'"

"I guess we shouldn't be surprised a fountain is getting us wet!"

"No, most of the surprises come when the fountains
are lit up at night."

"Where else should we go in Peru, Cayetana?"

"There is one place more special than all others,
but there are things to see on the way!"

"The city we came through is Cuzco and this is *Sacsayhuamán*. It was an Incan fortress. The Incas were the native settlers of Peru."

"It's huge!"

"How big are these stones?"

"Some weigh up to 125 tons."

"Wow!"

"Thousands of people come here every June for *Inti Raymi*, the Festival of the Sun."

"Hey, these are our first llamas! This is why we came here, Cayetana. We were curious about the llamas."

"They are everywhere, Molly. We'll see many more."

"The baby is so cute!"

"Do they use the fur to make clothes?"

"Generally, llama fur is used for rugs and wall hangings. It is much thicker than what is used for clothing."

"This is a traditional way of cooking. You make a fireplace of stones or dig a hole and once the fire is hot enough, you cook meat wrapped in banana leaves along with potatoes and fava beans."

"The potatoes and beans are right on top of the fire!"

"They are much easier to clean off, Molly.
The banana leaves protect the meat from the ashes."

"And the banana leaves don't burn up?"

"No, Michael. I don't know exactly why it works so well, but this method is very old."

"Oh, wow, the cloth is beautiful!"

"It is usually made of sheep or alpaca
    wool. Many different things are used
    to make the colors, including plants,
    tree bark, insects, even mold and
    sometimes rocks and minerals."

"Insects? Really?!"

"Yes, the *cochineal* is used
    for red, pink, and purple.

"It seems like no two things are alike."

"Everything is produced by hand.
    They could do the same thing
    over and over, but it's probably
    more fun to make something
    different."

"This dance is called a *huayno*. Here in the mountains they have a different word, *wayñu*, but it's pronounced the same. Here they use the Quechua word."

"'Why-no?' It's fun...and fast! What is the small guitar the band is using called?"

"It is the *charango* and it is made from an armadillo shell!"

"Oh my gosh!"

"Where are we, Cayetana?"

"This is *Aguas Calientes* and we are just a short distance away from the one place you must go when you come to Peru!"

"Welcome to Machu Picchu! This was an Incan settlement. It was abandoned in the 1500s when the Incas fought the Spanish. It was rediscovered in 1911."

"I can see how it got lost. It's amazing they built a whole town this high in the mountains."

"Just wait until you see the rest of it. We can see almost all of Machu Picchu from the hut."

"It's just incredible!"

"I saw pictures of this in a travel book. It looks big in photos, but really doesn't show just how huge the area is!"

"It is big. The archaeologists think that Machu Picchu was sort of a capital for this area. Of course it wouldn't be complete without llamas!"

"Hah-hah! Llamas always look like they're smiling."

"More of these beautiful clothes! I have to get
something to take home."

"Cayetana, you mentioned something about
a language called Quechua earlier."

"Yes, Michael. It is the language of the Andes Mountains.
It was the language of the Incas, and today there are still
eight million Quechua speakers. 'Llama' is a Quechua word."

"Are there any other words I would know?"

"Oh, yes. Of course there is the *alpaca*, which some people
mistake for llamas. Let's see, there's the grain *quinoa*, and
there are many other animals including the *puma* and *vicuña*."

"What do you think?"

"You look perfect, Molly. That is a very nice outfit."

"That's really cool, Molly."

"In Lima, we say *chévere* when something is 'cool.'"

"What does it mean?"

"Just what I said! When something is cool or nice, we say, *'Está chévere.'*"

"This corn is something. The kernels are big!"

"You say all of these are potatoes, Cayetana?"

"Yes, Molly. Peru has almost 4,000 types of potatoes."

"Whoa!"

"This is the famous Lake Titicaca. The country of Bolivia also borders it."

"What is this canoe made of?"

"It is a plant called *totora*. The island over there is also made of it."

"WHAT?!"

"Yes, there are nearly 50 of these islands. All of them have names. Some are big enough to have schools. They're called the *Islas del los Uros* after the Uro people."

"Floating islands? Wow!"

"This is another place not to be missed. We are at the *Canon del Colca*, or just 'Colca Canyon.' It's one of the deepest canyons in the world."

"I can't believe all these things we never knew about Peru. What are these birds, Cayetana?"

"These are Andean Condors, Molly. 'Condor' is another Quechua word, by the way. Some have wings that spread more than ten feet!"

"Did you see how it moved up and down without even flapping its wings?"

"We are now in the city of Arequipa and this is the
Monasterio de Santa Catalina. In English it is almost
the same name: Monastery of St. Catherine."

"The color is so rich, as deep as the blue we saw
in the other part of the monastery."

"Yes, Arequipa is a colorful city, much more than Lima
where we struggle with dust because of lack of rain.
But at least we don't have to worry about a volcano."

"Volcano?!"

"This is *Volcán Misti*. It last erupted in 1985. It is less than eleven miles away from here."

"That seems dangerous."

"They practice what will happen during an evacuation, but Arequipa has more than a million people. One neat thing is the animal preserve near the mountain. There is a pack of wild llamas there."

"*Está chévere!*"

"*Muy bien*, Michael!
'Very good.'"

"Cayetana, thank you for spending so much time with us. We learned so much!"

"It was fun for me too, Molly, but you haven't seen the beaches or the Amazon. There is so much more to see in Peru!"

"We'll have to come back sometime. I'd love to spend more time at Machu Picchu, too."

"You should come back for one of the festivals! Please keep in touch!"

"Thanks again!"

"Peru was amazing, Molly. I'm glad you wanted to learn more about llamas."

"We saw a lot of them, for sure. I thought they made clothes from the fur, but I guess not."

"Well, they sure were friendly, but more important, we made a new friend!"

"That is the best part of exploring new places—meeting new people."

LOOK FOR these OTHER titles in the SERIES!

MOLLY and the Magic Suitcase

Join Molly and Michael as they use their magic suitcase to learn about cultures, food, games, and landmarks around the world in this Readers' Favorite 5-Star book series.

Visit www.MollyAndTheMagicSuitcase.com for games and activities, and to learn more about the series. Follow Molly and the Magic Suitcase on Facebook for the latest news, events, and book releases.

ENJOY the FIRST Chapter bOOk with MOLLY and Michael!

MOLLY and Michael MYSTERIES

THE SHIELD OF HORATIUS

Marco Vittorini's family has a secret. For hundreds of years they protected the location of an ancient artifact. When Molly and Michael help Marco unravel a part of the puzzle, others take notice—including an unknown rival.

Simple curiosity leads to a race against time through the streets of Rome. The search takes them through churches, museums, and ruins. They witness an attack on the city through the words of a mysterious figure known as the Rescuer.

The three friends use every talent they have, but will it be enough? Join Molly and Michael for a mystery 2,500 years in the making.

Made in the USA
Charleston, SC
12 November 2014